Damien

RED ICE
DAMIEN CASEY
All work copyright Damien Casey 2023

Cover by Joe Fogle
Instagram -
@cryptoteeology

Damien Casey

FOR MARLI SIU THANKS FOR THE SONG

To those who don't know,
Put my book down and go watch
Anna and the Apocalypse
K THX

Prologue
Two Lives in Fast Forward

1952

The tiny flutter of insect wings fills a silent room. Four men watch on as their pride and joy takes his first jump. At the age of one, Lemuel, or Lemmy as Arthur calls him, has begun to develop his athletic side. He sprints across rooms, leaps into the air, his wings trying to keep his small body up but not quite up to the challenge of keeping rhythm.

Again, he jumps in place flapping back and forth. Again, he falls and whimpers when he can't levitate in the way his anatomy tells him he should.

"Was this a mistake?" asks one of the three men in black suits.

"No," says Arthur. "Not at all, he's barely a year old, Herb. He'll get there. Humans have an infancy, so why shouldn't he?"

"Because he's not exactly human… is he Arthur?"

Arthur shuts his eyes slowly. Anger forcing his face into a scowl. "He's human enough," he says before picking up Lemmy and holding him like an infant.

The small creature makes a sound like a cat purring. It runs its already talon sized claws across Arthur's jacket. It nuzzles its head against his chest and closes its eyes.

Behind the three men in suits, a radio comes to life and begins playing *Rudolph the Red-Nose Reindeer*.

"Christ," says one of the men. "It's July. Doesn't he like any other music?"

"Hey," says Arthur as he rubs Lemmy's head. "He likes Rudolph and Frosty. You should be happy that his echolocation works on electronics the way you hoped. Even if all he uses it for now is to tune into whatever radio station is playing his songs."

"Need to find that station. Shut 'em down for not knowing how to read a calendar."

The three men laugh and joke as they exit Lemmy's room.

Arthur lays Lemmy on his bed and covers him up.

He kisses his forehead and lets him sleep.

1960

"Ok, Lemmy," says Arthur. "I know this is scary for you. It's scary for me too. I don't like meeting new people either. But we've got to try this again, ok?"

Lemmy, now standing at five foot three, looks at Arthur with something akin to fear in his eyes. Arthur opens a door, and they walk into a brightly lit room.

Lemmy can't focus on anything except how bright the artificial lighting is; he covers his eyes

Red Ice

in shock and cries out.

"Goddamnit!" yells Arthur. "What did I tell you about the lights?"

"Sorry, sir," says a man in full army regalia. He flips a switch and the only lighting in the room is strings of Christmas lights.

Lemmy relaxes and walks around the room like a curious child. He flicks a green light with the tip of the talon on his right hand; the light flickers and Lemmy makes a sound like a giggle.

"It's disgusting," says a new voice entering from the door on the opposite side of the room. "Is THIS what you've been being paid for? Eight years, Arthur... eight years! Nothing to show for it except... this."

Lemmy can feel the man's disdain covering him like toxic waste shot from a hose. He scowls and shows three rows of razor-sharp teeth to the man. He unfurls his wings and slowly flaps them in a display of aggression.

"Arthur," says the man as he lights a cigarette. "You tell that son of a bitch to cool its jets or old Jones over here will light him up with grade A, government made, military issue gunfire. You get me?"

"Calm down, Lemmy," Arthur says as he rubs the side of his head. "It's ok." He clears his throat and begins to sing, "Rudolph the red-nosed reindeer... had a very shiny nose..."

Lemmy makes a sound like humming; he mimics the sounds of Arthur's singing.

"Well, isn't that just precious," says the man. "But how is this going to help us against the Russians? How is this going to end communism? All those secret files we got from the Nazis, and this is the best you can do. A singing… bug man."

"He's unlike anything to ever exist, Colonel," says Arthur. "He's the perfect blend of Man, Moth, and a few other traits from animals like bats. He can pinpoint and hunt down a single Fly in a wide-open space as big as fifteen miles with the same efficiency as a Great White Shark smelling blood. He's the perfect killer."

"Except for the part where he sings children's songs."

"Sir, he's barely just turned eight years old. There's still a large part of human DNA inside of him. It will take some time for him to reach adulthood."

"Speed it up."

"Despite how fast your mother rushed you into adulthood so you would be out of her life for good; I am unable to speed up the natural aging process-"

Arthur is pushed against the wall by the man. The Colonel pulls his sidearm and points it at Arthur's forehead.

"Don't you ever, EVER, speak to me like that-"

He's cut off as the lights go completely black. The walkie on the soldier's uniform begins to play a dissonant and distorted version of Rudolph.

"Arthur…" says the man.

The buzzing of insect wings fills the air.

The man is ripped away from Arthur faster than he can think. He's thrown across the table in the center of the room. His head rams into the stomach of the soldier who drops the gun.

"LEMMY! STOP!" yells Arthur.

The lights come back on.

The soldier is doubled over in pain clutching his stomach. Lemmy has the man Arthur called Colonel held above his head by his ankles. Lemmy's other hand is across the man's face. The talons piercing into the flesh as if he were going to take the man's face as a Halloween mask.

"Lemmy, put him down. I'm ok, you're ok. Let's let this one go, ok?"

Lemmy lifts the man up so that they're face to face. He growls and pulls his lips back.

The Colonel can feel the hot stench ridden breath as it coats him. He begins to breathe heavier and heavier as he counts each row of shark-like teeth inside this insect-shaped head.

One.

Two.

Three.

"Lemmy…"

Lemmy lets out a high-pitched wail and drops the man. He flies across the room and hides behind Arthur like a child.

"Alright, then," says the man. He stands up and begins dusting himself off. "We're going to need more of that. Only outside. Side by side with our men."

The two men leave the room. As the door closes, they hear Arthur singing while Lemmy hums along.

1963

Funding has shut down.

All assets are to be terminated.

All employees are to be paid for their silence.

One employee and one asset make their way through a system of drains that lead to a drainage ditch in the backwoods of Point Pleasant, West Virginia.

Together they make their way to the man's home.

His son was terrified at first saying there was a monster in his closet. His wife was so angry she almost left. After two days both could see how this "asset" was a living, breathing being with its own thoughts and feelings.

Together, on Christmas morning, mother and father watched as their biological and adopted sons opened gifts together.

1966

He's been allowed some freedom.

Some room to breathe and fly.

Red Ice

He's not supposed to leave the family's four acres, but how could he not?

He flies over the bunkers that used to function as storage for his old home.

He flies over cars driving along darkened backroads, none of which ever sees him.

He feels the air under his body; he watches the town of Point Pleasant as people move along in their simple lives.

He never knew what loneliness was until he was around other people.

He's woken up one morning by an angry Arthur. He's holding a newspaper with the headline, "couple claim to see 'Mothman' while driving."

The flights were supposed to stop then.

But Arthur can't take seeing Lemmy sad like that.

1967

The news reporter interviews a man:

"I swear on my life. I saw that Mothman thing dive down toward the water like it was hunting. There was something in that water he wanted. Something that came out of the bridge. That's the whole reason he destroyed it I bet."

"Thank you," says Arthur as he turns off the TV. He tips his head back and takes a long gulp of Whiskey. He runs his fingers across the note his wife left him about Christmas shopping. "I know you tried. And I thank you for that."

1972

Lemmy hides in the house just out of sight as the delivery boy leaves the groceries.

"You got any kids?" He asks.

"No," says Arthur. "Not anymore."

"I'm sorry."

1986

Arthur is taken away by a weird vehicle with red lights.

He told Lemmy to stay hidden downstairs until nightfall, then come up and eat.

1999

The world is in fear of some event called Y2K.

Arthur coughs up his drink and throws the bottle at the wall.

"Goddamn morons!" he yells.

Lemmy comforts the old man.

2008

"What could he have been? An astronaut? A doctor? I don't even care if he'd have been a fry cook. He could have done anything. Lemmy, I miss my son."

2014

Lemmy hides in the basement while his father cries again.

Red Ice

Arthur hates it when Lemmy sees him like this.

Lemmy hates that Arthur can't see he has a son right here.

A son begging for love and affection.

They both cry themselves to sleep on two different floors.

2023

"Lemmy!" yells Arthur from upstairs.

Lemmy turns his head from the freshly killed deer he's eating. He's had to fend for himself for the past couple of years; Arthur hasn't been able to look at him without crying. He hides in the basement, sneaks out at night to feed, and returns home to his father.

He opens the basement door and steps into the main room.

Arthur is close to death now. His age showing on his face. Lemmy still feels alive and youthful. He can move faster than any animal he encounters in the wild. He can hide better than the giant black cats he sees.

"Lemmy," Arthur mumbles. "Come over here, son."

Lemmy walks to the recliner.

A long metal device lay across Arthur's lap.

On the side table is the unfinished manuscript for the third book in a series about Lemmy he was writing.

Arthur had spent a few years earlier trying

as hard as he could to show Lemmy he wasn't the monster these bad movies made him out to be.

He could be kind.

He could help children.

The books didn't sell.

It broke Arthur's heart.

"Do you get it?" He said one morning seven years ago. "Arty is short for Arthur, and I created you like Dr. Arcane created the un-men."

Lemmy smiles at the memory, but then scowls as the third book sits unfinished, the same as it has for the past two years.

At some point Arthur gave up.

They stopped watching Nickelodeon and Cartoon Network together.

That's when Lemmy had to hide.

"I'm so sorry," says Arthur.

The TV shows the animated movie, *Rudolph the Red-Nosed Reindeer*.

"Sit down," he says. "Let's watch it together. I'm sorry I've been so cold the past couple years."

He begins to cry as he sings the song.

Lemmy places the old man's head against his chest and gums along.

Arthur places the end of the device against Lemmy's chest; right above his heart.

"I'm so sorry, son," he says as he pulls the trigger.

An explosion fills the room and Lemmy

Red Ice

stumbles backward in shock and pain. He runs his hands over the spot the bullet hit.

His pale white skin hasn't been punctured but a bruise develops.

Arthur watches as Lemmy's figure stands to full height. Nine foot tall, no fat to be found. Nothing but skin, bone, muscle, and now anger mixed with confusion.

Lemmy begins breathing faster.

His red eyes darting around the room.

Why did this happen?

Why did his father cause him this much pain?

Why does his heart hurt so badly when the bullet didn't touch it?

He lets out a shriek and flaps his wings fast.

He moves around the room quickly.

Arthur tries to reload the shotgun and aim again, as if the second attempt could pierce the skin that the first couldn't.

Lemmy stands before him, his body posture making the same display it did in that cold room so many years ago. He takes a slow and curious step toward Arthur.

The human parts completely erased now.

"I'm so sorry," Arthur says. "I love you."

He feels teeth pierce his neck and claws dig into his body.

He loses consciousness as the Christmas songs play in the background.

ONE
Christmas with a Monster

The car sputters and runs out of fumes just outside of the exit to Gallipolis, Ohio.

The chugging noise filling the small sedan fill with annoyance, dread, and I told you so.

"See," says Chris. "No car can go that long on E."

"I know my car," says Jessica.

"Apparently."

"It's just the air down here is different or something. All of these hills."

"Yeah, sure, totally. Makes sense. The hills and all."

"The Hills Have Eyes."

"Fuck off. I'm not in the mood for the game."

"My point anyway."

"Take it."

A large pickup pulls behind them. They can barely make out the color of the vehicle through the snowfall. The driver's side door opens and a man the size of a house gets out. He's at least six foot tall and two hundred with some change. He's wearing a flannel coat, blue jeans, and one of those hats with the flappy things on the side.

"Speaking of the Hills Have Eyes," says Chris.

Red Ice

Jessica shoots him a look that says, "hey, idiot, shut up or die."

The man taps on the driver's side glass. Jessica rolls the window down enough to speak, but not enough to let snow into the car that already has heating problems.

"Y'all ok?" The man asks. His accent is thick. Southern. He sounds like the romanticized version of Appalachia more than the stereotyped.

"Yeah," says Jessica. "We ran out of gas."

"Easy fix. I got a can I keep in my truck. It's full. Be back."

"Seems nice enough," says Jessica. "I told you this place would be nice."

"Let's just wait and see if the can is really full, or if he brings back a shotgun."

"Go ahead and start 'er up!" yells a voice from behind the car.

It makes Jessica jump.

She turns the ignition and the car sputters to life.

She rolls down the window to yell "thanks" and sees the man is standing at the window.

"Go on down this next exit, you'll have to get to the Speedway, I'm heading there before work if y'all want to follow me?"

"That would be amazing. Thank you."

They wait for the truck to pull off and Jessica pulls behind.

"Huh," says Chris. "Look at that. I guess I was afraid I'd see the confederate flag, not that."

He points to the bumper of the truck, barely visible is a pride flag sticker.

"See," says Jessica. "It's not as bad as you thought."

When they pull into the gas station, they see a truck covered in stickers that say things like, "ditch Joe and the hoe!" A huge confederate flag flies from a flagpole in the bed of the truck, the opposite side is a massive Trump 2024 flag.

"Ok," says Jessica. "Goddamnit."

She gets out to put gas in the tank; her plan is to avoid eye contact with whoever is driving that other truck.

"Thank you, so much," she says waving at the man who helped earlier. She notices his face for the first time while they're under the roof of the pump station. He's cute, he has a kind face. The kind of face you'd see in one of the many Hallmark movies she watches time and time again. Maybe this was her Christmas movie Christmas?

"Ain't no problem," he says. "Despite the message that chump is sending," he nods to the flag truck. "Not all of us are intolerant of human decency. My name's Lance. My friends call me Big L, because… well… I lose a lot."

They both laugh.

"Nah, it's because I'm big and my name starts with L. Anyway, what y'all doing down this way? Plates say Allen County."

"We're from Elida. I'm sort of a… don't

laugh… a Christmas fanatic. I saw Gallipolis has a great light display so we drove down for the weekend. I didn't think the snow would be this bad. My brother tagged along because he wants to go across the river to see Mothman stuff in Point Pleasant."

"Righteous. I can get behind it. A sibling road trip. Christmas with a monster."

"Yeah, I guess that's what it is."

"Well, I'll be late if I don't get going. I'm going to the lights tomorrow with my daughter. Maybe we'll see y'all there and say hi."

"Please do!"

They both give each other the awkward wave of two people who are smitten with each other. Jessica sits down in the Driver's seat and turns pure red.

"Are you going to fill the car up or just flirt for a bit and sit back down?" says Chris.

Jessica realizes with embarrassment she didn't even put gas in the car.

She gets out just in time to wave at Lance again as he laughs about her forgetting the gas. He pulls off and she starts the pump.

"You want a glizzy or anything?" Chris asks as he gets out of the car. "I need processed meat and electrolytes."

She shakes her head no.

She smiles as she looks around. The snow is covering everything. She's here with her brother. She met a decent guy.

Life was ok.

Damien Casey

TWO
A Dead Man in a Recliner

"Says the guy wrote kid's books? How long has he lived here? Never had him in town? The festival?" A police officer is talking to himself as he takes pictures of the scene. This particular officer, Jeff Morrison, has worked in Point Pleasant for close to twenty years.

When the millennium changed, so did he. From teacher to police officer. From classroom to car. He usually sits right off the bridge and catches speeders for nothing else than it annoys him how people come off the second bridge into town going fifty-five and zoom by McDonald's at fifty.

Two government guys showed up today. They told him their names were Ed and Ted. *Yeah, sure,* he thinks. These goons come in, smash up his scene, looking for some notebook. What notebook? It wasn't the guy's third book. That thing is on the ground half-finished and covered in blood.

The government guys come up the basement stairs shaking their heads. "Nothing but dusty family pictures down there," says Ed. "Looks like a deed deer got munched on by some dogs, but that's it."

"Well, Edward," says Jeff. "If you tell me what in the wide world of sports it IS you're looking for, I may be able to help."

"Can't tell you," says Ted.

"Ok then, Tedward," says Jeff. "This look interesting to you?"

He hands the man a drawing he found. Looks ancient. It's a crudely drawn little boy holding hands with a tall figure that looks like the world famous Mothman. The kicker? It's in a blank space on newspaper labeled, "you and your best friend!" with an address for kids to send their artwork. Dated 1964. Two years before the first Mothman story.

"No," says Ed. "Not interested in a dead man's heirlooms." Ed looks at the dead man, he shakes his head. "Goddamn. Sure would like to know what got in here. Place looks like it was ransacked by a panther. Got any zoos? Exotic animal dealers?"

"Used to have a fish store in town. Guy had giant fish in a kiddie pool. He had some weird stuff, but I don't think he had any panthers."

A young Police officer opens a cabinet. DVDs, VHS tapes, CDs, Cassette tapes, and records pour out.

"Goddamn it, Gerald," says Jeff.

"Guy sure loved his Christmas music," says Gerald.

All of the items are either *Rudolph the Red-Nosed Reindeer*, or *Frosty the Snowman*.

Gerald picks one up and looks it over, "older than me!"

"Gerald, put it back. They ain't even

making VCRs anymore."

Ed and Ted make eye contact and head outside. Jeff follows on their heels. They'll tell him something if it's the last thing he does.

"Got what you needed then?" Jeff asks.

"Nothing here," says Ted.

"Now listen, Tedward. I seen the way you both looked at that stuff. What happened? This guy create Christmas? Is that Santa Claus in there? What gives?"

"Not at liberty to say."

"Of course. At least tell me this; should I be on high alert?"

"Yes."

With that, Ted drops down into the passenger seat of the car. Gerald steps beside Jeff and they both watch as the car pulls off.

"Figure we should talk to the neighbor that called it in?" asks Gerald.

"Already did," says Jeff. "She said she noticed because the meat on the porch started to smell bad. Some animals had gotten into it. Said the guy was alone. Lost his wife and kid on the Silver Bridge."

"Jesus, he was old then?"

"Did you see him?"

"Yeah."

"Well, what do you think, Einstein?"

"Never been good at judging age."

"Yeah? You good at judging animal prints?"

Jeff points to a spot of mud and snow with a deep three toed imprint. In front of each toe is a slash mark; the look of a pissed-off big cat.

"That's a dinosaur," says Gerald, "sure as shit. That or some sort of deranged Sasquatch."

Jeff squats down and takes a few pictures with his phone.

"Got a hunch that THIS is what them suits were after," Jeff says before heading to his car and leaving.

THREE
Death of a Saleswoman

A cordless phone is ringing off the hook in a storefront. Ashley is the only person who hasn't left town it seems. Probably her husband calling to tell her about some rumored snowstorm.

Who decided a cordless phone was a good idea? she thinks, *are we thirteen?*

She finds it in time for the caller to hang up. *Of course*, she thinks, *my luck would be I won The Lottery; even more my luck, it would be the Shirley Jackson kind.* She starts to redial the number when the electricity goes out.

Heavy snow on weak power lines can only mean one thing, a power outage.

She goes behind the counter and finds her cell phone. She sends a text that bounces back due to lack of signal.

She shakes it back and forth in her hand as if that will solve the problem of Point Pleasant being a dead zone for her carrier. Sometimes saving twenty bucks a month isn't worth all of this. That's what she told her mother, but her mother didn't care. Twenty bucks was twenty bucks and who the hell was Ashley to tell her how to spend her money anyway?

Something thuds against the front door causing her to jump. Too many stupid ass movies. That's what her husband said. I'll thank you to not be so nosey about what I watch at the store on my own Netflix account thank you very much.

The outline of a figure is leaning against the door. It takes her breath away for a moment before she remembers it's the wooden Mothman. The lights wouldn't be getting any power, so she couldn't see the Christmas lights wrapped around it. The only thing that gave it away was the outline of the Santa hat on its head.

"This is all your fault, you know?" she says to the wooden face pressed against the window. She opens the door and steps out into the small alcove. On her right, a brick wall, on her left, the sidewalk and then the snow-covered road.

She watches the snow falling in the darkness. *It really is getting bad*, she thinks. She looks up and down the street; the only cars visible are covered in snow. The owners must have gone home some other way.

If she gets stuck in town at least she has that sleeping bag in her car she's been forgetting to get out for six months. She thinks a bed would be better than a sleeping bag on carpet covered concrete; but the idea of staying in the supposedly haunted Lowe hotel isn't that appealing to her, even if she could for free.

Keith would be working tonight, that would for sure be a free stay. But is it worth it? All the

Red Ice

stories he told her of seeing people slightly out of focus.

Nope.
Definitely not messing with ghosts.
Give me something I can punch, kick, or stab.
Not an invisible thing walking through walls.

She hears the snow crunching down the road. A tall and lanky person is walking toward her. Their coat wrapped around their body so that all she can make out is a vague egg like shape.

From inside her pocket, her phone begins playing *Rudolph the Red-Nosed Reindeer*. She pulls it out and sees that there aren't even any apps open. The figure has stopped walking and now just stares at her.

The snow-covered cars up and down the road come to life. Their radios in sync with her phone, the music playing so loud it could be coming from the sky.

Ashley says, "nope," and jumps back into her store in a hurry. She slams the door and locks it. When she turns around two red eyes are staring at her. She screams and throws a punch; her fist connects with a plush Mothman that fell from a shelf thanks to the force of the slammed door.

She slams the thing down and kicks it.

She hears a scratching on the storefront window. When she turns, another set of red eyes are staring in at her. The claws that remind her of the time she was told to Google Ostrich talons lightly run along the window.

All of the music stops.

The night is quiet finally.

The figure stares inside.

She walks up to the window thinking someone is playing a really bad prank on her. Maybe this is the comeback episode of that show on MTV where they set up scary situations and dropped innocent bystanders into them. She cracks a smile thinking of the episode with the rat-man. She puts her face close to the window and still can't make out any details in the costume other than it has to be filled with the skinniest person alive to be a suit and still look like a man who hasn't eaten in seven years.

The wings open, making her jump. This is the moment she realizes it's definitely a prank.

She laughs and pulls out her phone. She points it at the guy's face and takes a picture with the flash on.

What she sees is the face of a demon. Two red eyes grow, a mouth with three rows of shark-like teeth opens wide and lets out a shriek. The figure leaps into the air and vanishes. The electricity in her building flashes back on. Every tv, speaker, and radio begins playing *Frosty the Snowman*.

The front window explodes sending glass and snow everywhere. Ashley falls over a display of Mothman merchandise and crawls backward on the palms of her hand. The song drones on like a children's play in town of madmen. The thing stands there like a tree made of flesh; completely still.

The song slows down and fades away as it walks toward her. Its footfall makes no noise at all. It reaches its claws out toward Ashley's screaming face to silence her and protect itself from the blinding light that caused it pain.

***

In the Lowe Hotel, a man named Keith hears the screaming of a woman. *First the blackout, now this?* He thinks. *Yeah, this place is haunted AF.*

FOUR
Lights on Trees

"Oh great, it's your friend and mine," says Chris nodding at an approaching Lance. Lance is jogging toward them with his arms flailing. A little girl with pigtails sits on his shoulders holding onto his chin for dear life. She's wearing a huge puffy pink jacket and teal pants that match in puffiness.

"Stop!" says Jessica nudging him. "He's nice, and kind of adorable. Look how he's carrying his daughter."

Jessica and Chris showed up in Gallipolis about an hour ago. They checked into a hotel, ate at the pizza place across the road that was recommended. It was called Larobi's and it had a nice layer of grease sitting atop the cheese. The best pizza, in Chris' opinion, has to have that layer of grease.

"My stomach is killing me," Chris said when they pulled up to the park.

"You ate three fourths of that thing," said Jessica.

They walked into stores, looking around, waiting for night. Chris kept grabbing his stomach and groaning. At some point, Jessica found herself drinking a beer by herself and waiting on Chris.

She felt a shadow looming over her and

Red Ice

looked up. When she turned around, there was a man there holding out a business card.

"And you are?" He said.

"Does this work usually?" She asked.

"Yeah, I got a job. I got some money. What's not to work?"

"Awful thin business card."

"You got a business card?"

"Apparently I don't need one."

"Can I get you a drink?"

"No."

"What the fuck?"

"If your strategy is to show girls a business card for your... yep... Nationwide office... I'm going to continue to enjoy this draft Newcastle alone."

"Maybe I just wanted to chat?"

"You thought that business card was like a credit card, and you were buying a one-way ticket into my pants, didn't you?"

"Fuckin' bitch."

"There it is!"

"Hey, Randall!" Said the bartender. "Leave the customers alone. I already told you it'd get you banned."

Randall nodded at the bartender, then flipped him the bird before taking his Bud Light back over to his four friends playing pool. They all laughed at him.

"Watch yourself, ma'm," said the bartender. "Guys like those don't like getting laughed at. Never grew up past being a high school quarterback."

"No worries," Jessica said. "I've dealt with worse."

When Chris finally came out, they had another beer. She told Chris what happened and then sent an Amaretto Sour with a little pink umbrella over to Randall. Jessica waved and winked at him on her way out. If looks could kill, the way Randall looked at them he would be charged for double homicide.

"Yeah," says Chris. "After you decided to piss off the southern Ohio insurance mafia, we may need Lance around."

Jessica rolls her eyes.

When Lance reaches them, he introduces his daughter, Camory.

"Don't be mad at my dad," she says shrugging. "My mom made up my name. She says it's a car and the name of her dad combined. But I don't get that. Her dad's name is grandpa."

They all laugh as Lance explains to Camory how her grandpa has a different name to her mom.

Chris and Jessica introduce themselves and have to wait for the little girl to take of her blue mittens before they can shake hands.

"I'm eight," Camory says. "I can dress myself now." She does a little spin so that Jessica and Chris can appreciate her choice of wardrobe.

"She's kind of an attention hog," says

Red Ice

Lance. "How y'all like the lights?"

"Love them!" says Jessica. She didn't want to go into the deep details about how this small-town park covered in Christmas lights made her feel like she was in a movie. She sips her hot chocolate and smiles. Lance catches her eye and smiles back.

"How long y'all in town for?" Lance asks

"Three nights," says Chris. "She wants to come to these dumb lights all three nights and leave on Monday. It's Friday, Lance. Friday."

"Well, how would you like to go check out the lights across the river? Maybe some Mothman stuff?"

"Sure," says Jessica looking at Chris. "We can meet you there."

"Nah, I got the good car, not my work truck. I'll drive y'all."

They head to Lance's car without any idea of the five men following behind them that are still pissed off about a little umbrella in an amaretto sour.

FIVE
Intruder

The mid two thousands were filled with a trend of gender specific hangout areas. Man caves and she sheds overtook the land. There wasn't a glowing beer sign or shade of pink that was safe.

Jeff thinks about the time his wife, Nan, tried to get him to move all of his stuff into a spare room. She kept doctoring up what she wanted to say, "get your shit out of the living room," as, "won't it be nice to have a MAN CAVE?"

To Jeff, a den of masculinity was a little unnecessary. When asked, Nan said it would be a cool place for Jeff and Gerald to hang out and talk about sports. Jeff informed her he spends twelve hours a day, five days a week with Gerald. He sees Gerald more than his wife, kids, or grand babies. Gerald doesn't even like sports unless you count chasing uninterested women around at Courtside a sport. Of course, he has to compete with a meathead like Randall King in that Olympic sport. Gerald is the nice one who wants to take women to little country concerts and be all romantic over a picnic on the riverfront with burgers from First and Main. He won't listen to Jeff about the kind of women that choose Randall over Gerald. The

Red Ice

kind of women Gerald keeps chasing would rather get a five-course meal at Applebee's and listen to a loudmouth asshole like Randall talk about Trump exposing the truth behind reptilians in the White House. Women can be meatheads too, and meatheads tend to congregate together.

Gerald is too smart to find romance in a red state.

That's what Nan always says when the subject comes up.

Another reason he didn't want the goddamn man cave. Randall was all the time running his mouth about having one. Son of a bitch is single; shouldn't his whole house be a man cave?

Fuck it, Jeff thinks. *At least this woman got a shed to keep her sanity in.* Poor Rhonda Stewart went off and married her high school sweetheart. They seem happy enough, but Lane Stewart couldn't find the word brain if it were painted neon green on a hot pink flip-flop and set atop a bowl of brown M&Ms. When Lane was a teen, he wrote one fourth for the answer to five divided by one. When Jeff asked how he got there, Lane said he walked. Dumb bastard didn't know he meant how he got to the answer, he thought Jeff was asking how he got to school.

Good thing Rhonda handles the bills and Lane handles the love, Jeff thinks. One thing the boy could do was care about someone. This much was proven right now as he followed Jeff and Gerald with a rifle to Rhonda's she shed.

"See," Lane whispers. "Told you the son of a bitch was in there."

They walk through the snow; the white being illuminated by the blinking red and green of the lights hanging from the shed. They hear a low whining, like someone is crying and gasping for air. Definitely a kid who's scared now that they're caught. No one else would be crying like that while they're trying to hide.

The call came across ten minutes ago. Lane said he saw a fully grown man leap out of his kitchen window with armloads of stuff. He didn't let his boy, Malcolm, or Rhonda get out of the car. Rhonda was annoyed, claiming that the giant light up snowman that could be seen from space was the issue. Someone probably thought they were rich. Lane said it was probably the shed covered in Christmas lights. Either way, Rhonda and Malcolm are still sitting there with the heat on. Lane called as he got his rifle from his hunting truck. When he went into the backyard, he heard the crying.

"What kind of a prick steals something and then cries about it in a shed?" asks Gerald. "Why does your wife even have this shed anyway? Ain't she sheds supposed to be pink?"

"It's for her scrapbooking business. More of a workshop. Plus, it works nice as a guest bedroom."

"Be a real bastard to have to take a crap

staying the night with you all."

"Hey," says Jeff waving his hands at them. "Shut the fuck up."

Lane and Gerald shrug their shoulders and laugh silently about Jeff's attitude.

"Rhonda's sister ever stay with y'all?" Gerald asks.

Whoever is in the shed hears Gerald's question and stops crying. They must realize they've been found and finally decide that silence and hiding should always be a pair.

The sound of a large dog growling comes from behind the door.

"Fuck me," says Gerald.

Loud banging fills the night air. The sound of heavy fists against a wooden wall. They hear the window on the backside of the shed shatter. Splintered wood thudding into snow covered ground is the soundtrack to them moving faster to the door.

When they throw it open, no one is there. The far wall has completely fallen down. The woods behind can be seen like looking out an open garage door. They see the trees moving and hear branches breaking. The sound moves through the trees and up into the sky as if whoever it was had a rocket strapped to their back.

Jeff runs to the tree line and stops. He thinks about what whoever did that to a wall could do to his head if they met. He looks down and sees the same three toed foot prints as earlier.

"Jeff…"

He turns to see what Gerald and Lane are looking at.

On the day bed, stuffed reindeer with red noses and snowmen with wooden pipes lay in a pile. Some on the ground beside the bed look like they got thrown when whatever that was stood up and ran.

"Bastard only stole Christmas stuff," says Lane.

"I told you you didn't build that wall right," says Rhonda from the doorway.

All three men jump, her appearance scaring the hell out of them.

"Rhonda," Lane says. "I told you to stay in the truck!"

"I didn't want my she shed to get shot all to hell, but it looks like you didn't need to. Your shitty carpenter skills did that."

"What's this?" asks Malcolm picking at something black and wet in the doorway.

"Don't touch that!" Lane says. "Can I take them inside, y'all?"

Gerald and Jeff nod.

"Damn thing is wet," Gerald says while picking up a stuffed Rudolph. "Wall ain't been busted that long."

"Nope," says Jeff. "We heard crying, remember? Those are tears."

SIX
Mud

Lance feels his feet sinking deeper into the mud as he holds his weight and Camry's. He can't believe her fifty pounds is enough to make that much of a difference, but it is. He wonders if he's just telling himself that so that he feels better about the situation his shoes are going through. At some points he can feel the mood ooze over the top and slide into his sock. The snow melting and forming a weird muddy slop isn't helping his case either. If anything, that's just making his minutes feel worse.

He's hoping Jessica isn't mad about the mess; her brother isn't at all. If Jessica is, that could ruin any chance that Lance has for dinner and a movie. *Look how presumptuous you're being*, he thinks. *This girl could have a boyfriend or girlfriend back home and not want me trying to slide into her real-life DMs.* Lance continues to mentally berate himself for a crime no one else even knows he committed.

"Hey, Jess," says Camry. "Do you have a boyyyyyyfirend?"

"I don't," says Jessica. "Us women don't need boyfriends to be happy, do we?"

"I don't think I'm old enough to answer that."

"Is that it?" Chris asks pointing off to the

right. He shook his head at the cutesy little kid talk. Uncovering the mysteries at hand are his concern. In his mind, he's going to solve the Cryptid case that's plagued humanity for decades by going into a bunker.

There's a big white dome covered in snow and dead tree branches. A small entrance is in the front and Lance nods a yes.

Chris charges ahead into the former bunker. Lance stumbles along behind him, awkwardly breaking sticks. He hands Camry off to Jessica who sets the girl down on the dry ground.

"What'd they keep in here?" Chris asks.

"Nothing really," says Lance. "Or at least nothing I know of."

Lance's phone rings. It's the theme song from *The Exorcist*.

"That's mom," Camry says. "She probably wants to make sure I'm in bed and NOT in a weird scary place with strangers."

"Yeah, well," says Lance. "Maybe she shouldn't have been in a weird scary bed with strangers."

"I think I'm too young to hear that, dad!"

Camry immediately runs over to a spray-painted pentagram made out of crudely drawn parts of the male genitalia.

"What's this?" She asks.

"It's an ancient symbol," says Jessica turning Camry away from the image. "It means teenage boys are immature little turds."

Chris takes photos, the flash from his phone

Red Ice

lighting up thousands of pictures of the Mothman painted inside the dome.

"Do you think he lived here?" Chris asks.

"No," says Lance. "I think he never lived anywhere. It wasn't real."

"A non-believer? In the homeland?"

"Sorry, friend. I think it was an owl or a stork. Probably a big bird."

"See," says Jessica. "Told you it was just a crane."

"I think he was a government experiment," Chris says. "I think they were meddling around like that book about the super smart dog and the monster."

"That's a new one," says Lance. "About the dog."

"Dad told me I could get a dog," says Camry. "Just as long as I take it out when I'm there."

"That's reasonable," says Jessica.

Jessica shines the light from her phone on a picture that's been taped to the wall. It shows two young girls with black eyes standing beside a thing that can only be described as a mutated pig. The thing is small and pinkish, it looks like it has double the amount of skin it needs.

Below is another picture. This picture looks to be the backside of the one above it. In cursive it reads, "the girls and their pet, the Squonk." A piece of paper taped below reads, "another genetic experiment. Found this at the same place I found this picture of the

Mothman," there's an arrow that points to a blank space on the wall. "Found it in the old man's house when we broke in."

"Spooky spaghetti," Lance says coming up beside her.

"Do you mean creepy pasta?" she asks.

"Yeah, kid's make this stuff up and tape it all over the walls in here. That poor little pig or whatever it is. Being forced to hang out with these two emo girls."

"That's real," Chris says. "I told you it was government experiments."

Lights fill the dome. The headlights of a car doing a slow turn as its lights shine into the dome. They hear a car door slam and voices follow yelling about knowing that's where that bitch was going. Camry steps behind Lance and holds his pant leg.

"I think I'm too young to hear that," she says.

"Sometimes teenage boys aren't the only immature little turds," says Jessica.

They see flashlights lighting up the ground outside. A figure fills the doorway.

"Boo," he says shining his light into his face.

Randall.

"You're an immature little turd," says Camry.

Randall cracks a smile.

"Bringing your kid for protection, lance?" says Randall.

"I don't know what I'd need protecting

Red Ice

from," says Lance.

"Your little girl embarrassed me at Court Side."

"Sorry, I don't think Camry is old enough to go there."

"Your grown-up girl."

"Only got the one daughter."

"You know damn well who I'm talking about."

"Yeah? Well, I don't own her. I think of women a little differently than you. More like they're human beings and not some porcelain doll that you show around town."

Randall stares at Lance.

Lance can tell he wants to hit him.

"None the less," says Lance. "Doesn't look like you're taking care of anything here, does it?"

"I guess not," says Randall as he backs out of the dome. "I guess I'll see y'all around later."

They hear the car pull off. The tires shooting mud in all directions.

"I thought I had to worry about the Mothman killing me tonight," says Chris.

"Just an immature turd," says Camry.

SEVEN
Thanks for the Follow

His inner thighs were starting to chafe and there wasn't a single damn thing he could do about it. The live was going phenomenal and the cash money was rolling in. He knew what he had to do as soon as he saw the power go out.

The camera wouldn't be working so he could set up his tripod and go live in front of the Mothman statue. This time, he wrapped it in battery powered Christmas lights. He threw on his Santa hat and started streaming. A little festive cheer was bound to get him some views. He watched one guy pretend to be Santa who got more gifts in an hour than the real Santa passed out on Christmas night. *This NPC shit is too easy*, he thinks.

He found out about the trend of being a NPC, a non playable character, on TikTok when this babe dressed as Princess Zelda popped up on his feed. At first, he was interested in her tits and cute little pointy ears. He didn't remember a Zelda game where Zelda was that stacked and showing that much skin. He thought that was more Purah in *Tears of the Kingdom* than Princess Zelda. He watched as the gifts rolled in and all she did was do the same phrase and motion over and over again. It was literally like someone was spamming a button on a video game.

So, there he was, idea in head. He made up a character; some D&D bullshit, got an account, and let the money roll in. He bought a cheao dragon horn at Spirit Halloween and paired it with a spray-painted shield. He threw on a dollar bin suit of armor and VOILA, the birth of Rian the Revenge.

He knew being in front of the statue would make bank. People fucking love the Mothman ever since that Fallout game. The festival was huge this past year so why not capitalize on it? If anything, maybe he would gain some followers.

The last time he tried to film here, that son of a bitch came out and ran him off. Must have seen him on the live camera the guy has pointed at the statue for out of towners. He came out all pissed-off about the view being ruined. Like, what view? It's filmed from the side of a building.

Dweeb wouldn't even take a percentage.

"Ho Ho horny!" He says as he runs his hand along the horn taped to his head.

The gifts roll in.

"Ho Ho horny! Ho Ho horny! I'm hungry! Thanks for the rose! Thanks for the rose! Lighting! Lightning! Ho Ho horny!"

He'd do this for an hour and then he'd turn the thing off and cash in.

Rian wasn't lucky enough to have parents

who knew how to spell Ryan, and he wasn't lucky enough to be born in NYC or somewhere that these gigs get more views, but he knew how to do it when he was getting viewers. He turned his charisma up and got all these goofs sending him rose after rose after rose after lightning bolt.

He stood there rocking back and forth; in loading screen stance. He always had a default stance for when he didn't receive gifts. These were usually the moments people tried to get him to break character. He always said he would at a certain point, a point that wasn't possible to reach.

"Ho Ho horny!" He says as another gift rolls in.

He watches the chat for a bit as he continues his act.

> Dudes a loser.
> Who watches this shit?
> There's something flying around behind you.
> Fuck these NPC guys.
> This is the future of America.
> Dude, something is back there.

"Ho Ho horny!"

> This is the worst cosplay.
> He has a horn and a scale vest, that makes

Red Ice

him?

"Ho Ho horny! Thanks for the rose! Lightning! Lightning! Oh! It's corn!"

Looks like red eyes.

"Ho Ho horny! Thanks for the rose! Thanks for the rose! It's corn! It's corn! Oh! Oh! Oh!"

Dudes out of his mind.
Doesn't he see the guy in a costume?
Yo he behind you bitch

That last one catches his eye. He breaks character and spins around. Behind him is a massive figure. It's taller than him by a couple feet but thinner. It has saliva running from its mouth as its glowing red eyes stare at him. He breathes in so hard he feels like his ribs are going to snap.

All the power in town flashes back on and he sees the face as clear as day in the lights pointing at the statue. It's like looking at the real-life version of Bigfoot next to a wooden carving. This is the Mothman, absolutely it is, but this thing looks a lot more dangerous than the metal statue. Nothing about what he's looking at would make a good plush toy. This is a thing that should be hidden in a basement, not celebrated yearly. This isn't the ideal mascot for pancakes at a festival in September. They've all been wrong. This thing is real and not totes adorbs.

Rian screams in its face and it does the same. He feels his face coated in hot saliva. It leaps into the air and flies away. He finishes screaming as he feels the cold air from the thing's updraft. He stans in shock. Then he remembers his phone has been sending this live feed out into the world. This is the break he needs. Maybe someone filmed it. Either way, this is going to make him a ton of cash.

"Holy fucking-" he starts to say. His dreams of hot tubs and girls dressed as Purah AND Princess Zelda fill his mind.

When he turns to grab his phone, two massive feet hit him in the chest. He's lifted by the three clawed toes on each foot. He feels talons puncturing through his fake armor and into his flesh. He hears his right shoulder begin to shatter and feels his left dislocate.

He feels a sharp pain in his back that goes all the way through his chest. He reaches down and feels the hand of the statue protruding straight through him. Pieces of rib cage and chunks of flesh are in the snow below him. He hears a car radio playing *Rudolph the Red-Nosed Reindeer* while at the same time his phone starts playing *Frosty the Snowman*.

The lights go out in town again and he

Red Ice

stays pinned to the statue, the blinking glow of Christmas lights allowing his followers to keep watching.

> Guys a fraud.
> Oh great a new hoax.
> Ho ho hoax you mean!
> How long is he going to stay there?
> Y wuz he playin frosty????
> I'm leaving.
> Same.
> Totes
> Boring AF
> FUCK THIS GUY.

Five minutes later, he takes his last breath as his live plays to zero people.

Damien Casey

EIGHT
Found Footage

The worst haunted house Gerald had ever gone to was in a town called Middleport about a half hour away. It was run by these weird Christian people in a church that had caught fire. They rebuilt it but did it all wrong. They apparently didn't put enough braces in or something because when Gerald and his friends went the thing had a bow in the middle of the second floor. Like there was too much weight in the middle. The steps going up had a sort of lean to them that didn't feel safe at all.

When he got into the haunted house there were all sorts of things that were supposed to make you feel as though you were in Hell. He couldn't ever figure out what a knock off Leatherface or an alien had to do with Hell, but three out of five friends got "saved" that night.

He thinks back to that night as he walks up this rickety stair set at midnight. He starts laughing to himself about his friend, Trey, who said he knew for a fact that Hell was just a giant butcher shop where souls got chopped up and sold to demons.

Last year Gerald found Trey dead in a ditch down by Carson farm. Two bullet holes in his chest and a reputation for dealing with some pretty nasty heroin dealers.

Red Ice

As usual, God was nowhere to be found at that scene. Jesus wasn't cleaning up the blood on the road. The Holy Spirit wasn't helping find the killers.

The church to drugs to church to gambling to church pipeline was going strong and taking lives before they ever went into one of those coffee shops that only has coffee from a Keurig.

Jeff knocks on Jimmy's door and pulls him out of his thoughts. They hear shuffling on the other side and the clatter of junk falling from somewhere high up.

"Shit!" Says a voice inside. "Goddamn it! Who is it anyway?"

"It's Jeff and Gerald," says Jeff.

"Well?"

"You tell me."

"I ain't got a thing to tell y'all."

"Why'd you call us then?"

"I called?"

"Damnit, Jim," says Gerald. "Stop bullshitting around and let us in."

The door opens and three cats run out. The smell of cat pee hits Gerald's nose like a haymaker from Tyson. He feels himself reeling and grabs ahold of the handrail to steady himself. Jeff grabs his shoulder and coughs, the smell getting to him too.

"God!" Says Jeff. "Why haven't you sprayed some Febreeze or something?"

"What'd'ya mean?" asks Jimmy. "Come in.

Check this out."

Gerald looks back at the stairs and contemplates following the cats to clean air. Instead, he strolls in and stands next to Jeff in the kitchen side of the kitchen/living room combo apartment.

"Come sit down," Jimmy says. "Want a Ski or anything?"

"Nah," says Gerald. "Shit tastes like a pound of boiled worms in battery acid."

Jimmy shrugs and pulls a can from the case on the coffee table. It feels like a stuffy closet during a heatwave in here and smells like a gas leak mixed with a crashed kerosene truck. Gerald thinks to ask what Jimmy has the heat turned up to, but he wants to get out of here quick.

Jimmy pushes a few buttons on a remote and a small TV sitting in front of a 65 inch comes to life. It shows a live feed of the Mothman statue. Jimmy bought a little security camera system so he could broadcast to the world from his apartment. He put a donation option on his site and hasn't missed rent in two years.

"Here," he says. "Check this shit out."

The camera blinks and there's a giant bird flapping its wings in front of the statue. It flies away and leaves behind a man. The man is pinned to the statue. A metal arm going through the guy's back and out of his chest.

"Can't tell if it's real," Jimmy says. "Rian is

Red Ice

always trying to make a cheap buck, so it may be a fraud."

"Have you, now here's just a suggestion," says Gerald, "actually looked to see if he's still pinned up? Or is this a thing you're both making?"

"Too scared to look."

"Damn..." Jeff says standing by the window that looks out toward the statue. "Guy's dead as can be."

Gerald steps up beside Jeff and looks out the window. Sure enough, there's Rian pinned up like some weird, haunted house ornament. Gerald tries to think of a way those weird Jesus people would turn this into something about Hell.

Neither man says a word as they make their way out of the door and down a less terrifying set of stairs. They walk over to Rian, and both shake their heads.

The phone is still broadcasting to TikTok.

"He was doing that video game thing," says Gerald. He takes the phone from the tripod and turns it off.

"Santa hat was locked on there good," says Jeff. He turns from the body and makes a call. Gerald assumes it's to get someone to come clean up the body.

He looks at the frozen blood on the ground. He thinks about the video he just saw. He pulls out his phone and opens TikTok.

"Jeff..." he says as he sees the first video.

Damien Casey

NINE
Kidz Bop Live

After fifteen times of Meghan Trainor's version of *White Christmas* being sung, or screamed, by an eight-year-old, Lance is usually about ready to pound his head against a cobblestone road in 1874 until he needs a lobotomy. Fortunately, Camry is showing off for new people and letting "A Very Trainor Christmas" play straight through. When it isn't Christmas, it's that custom playlist of every song, every version of every song, and every single remix of every song. There is a Meghan Trainor supremacy in Lance's car whenever Camry was around.

Other kids liked Jojo or whatever, a couple different things. Not Camry. All she wanted to do was listen to the same twelve Meghan Trainor tracks over and over again until simply hearing the name was an insult to Lance's ears. Would it kill her to start listening to at least one other singer? Just one?

He's worn out by Meghan Trainor.

Camry sings in the back seat. She's sitting beside Chris as he tries to play along. Jessica is up front; she isn't missing a single beat of the songs. If anything, this is encouraging Camry to keep singing the same song over and over and over and over. Jessica doesn't know that.

She won't either until all of a sudden, she's found the unique mixture of doo wop and modern pop that M-Train produces just as boring and same old same old as a local hardcore band who discovered open notes and testosterone.

"Can we listen to something else?" Lance says. "It's all start in' to run together."

"No!" yells Camry.

"Come on," says Jessica. "What's not to love about her quirky lyrics and upbeat music with a deeper message?"

"Most people couldn't catch a deeper meaning if it were the ocean, and they were a fish."

"Metaphors aren't really your strong point, are they?"

"Not anyone else in the world's either. They stay on the surface."

"Hey, sometimes a werewolf book is just a werewolf book."

"Not a study of loneliness?"

"Whatever you nerds are talking about," says Chris. "It's getting gross."

"I think they're flirting," Camry says while giggling.

"Not very good at it, are they?"

"No!"

"What the…" says Lance.

Two red dots in the road ahead move faster and faster toward them. Lance thinks it's a car in park until it starts getting closer. When the

Red Ice

lights get closer, he thinks it's a car in reverse. The lights lift into the air and fly out of sight. The playlist skips forward to Meghan's version of *Rudolph the Red-Nosed Reindeer*. The volume in the car turns up, Lance turns the nob down and nothing happens.

"It's broken," Lance says.

"Are we just not going to talk about that UFO?" asks Chris.

Lance pushes the power button on the stereo to get the song to stop and nothing happens. The whole set fades in and out. Crackles emit from the speakers like crunching snow. The song returns to the previous track at a reasonable volume.

"UFOs can't control radios," says Chris. "Especially not one like that."

"That was a flying person," says Camry. "His little feet were hanging there."

"I saw a body too," says Jessica.

They drive in silence thinking about how a fun night has turned into horror. The novelty of going to see a monster turned into the very real fear of a monster flying above them.

The radio crackles again and begins playing a classic version of *Frosty the Snowman*. Something thuds against the roof of the car. Camry screams as two talons scratch along the window beside her.

Bright lights from a car behind them make them all blink. They hear a scream, the song changes, and then they hear a loud crash.

Damien Casey

The car rides on two wheels along the side of the road. Just barely keeping out of a ditch.

They all scream as the car loses balance and falls sideways into the small ravine. Glass shatters, the sound of folding metal.

"Is everyone ok?" Lance asks as he spins around to grab Candy.

"Daddy!" Camry yells in fear.

They hear voices and footfalls coming through the snow.

"The hell was that?"

"Some sort of bat!"

"Giant ass bird!"

"You see! I was trying to show you that TikTok about Rian!"

The passenger side door opens, and a hand reaches in.

Jessica is pulled from the wreckage and sees Chris climbing out behind her.

She looks up to thank her rescuer.

Randall.

TEN
A Viral Sensation

Death and sex have one thing in common. People love watching it happen. Cleaning up the mess? That's someone else's gig. There's something about knowing death is in our future, and getting to see it play out on someone else that fascinates people. Everyone knows that's what waits for them, but to get a little snapshot? To maybe prepare oneself a little? Isn't that priceless?

It's one in the morning and the pajama brigade is out in full effect trying to catch a glimpse of a dead guy on a statue.

It doesn't matter what kind of phone Rian used. It doesn't matter where he lived. It doesn't matter who he knew.

Right now, his corpse is a window giving a view that alleviates some fears for a few minutes. A window to peak in and say, "huh, I guess maybe that ain't all bad."

Or maybe humanity as a whole is just a little blood thirsty?

Either way is a bullshit excuse to Jeff. People dragging their kids out of bed to look at this Christmas tree that looks like it came straight out of *The Texas Chainsaw Massacre*.

The worst part is Rian's jaw had been ripped open so badly that it just hung there all disconnected like a broken toy and open for business like that shark in front of the aquarium Jeff's grandkids forced him to go into. He realized getting eaten by a giant shark was sort of a phobia of his that day.

Isn't that one of everyone's phobias?

Somehow a string of lights had gotten tangled up in the gory mess of Rian's body and a bright green one was sitting inside the cage of his mouth. Between that light and the bloodstained snow, Rian could have been a Christmas ornament sold at Spirit Halloween.

"You ever wonder about the karmic implications of all this?" asks Gerald.

"I figure people lined up to see Jesus pinned up like that," Jeff says. "Rian should be so privileged."

"Sad way of looking at it."

"Only way of looking at it that doesn't piss me off."

Gerald nods along to that. Sure, why not?

They drive past the packed street. As they pass Domino's they see two people in uniforms locking up and looking in that direction. Jeff slows the car down.

"Go the hell home you morbid losers," he yells out the window after flashing the siren lights.

"Phones ringing," says Gerald.

Jeff looks down and the screen reads "unkown" with the number 0 as the phone number.

Red Ice

Something tells him to answer this time. He's not sure exactly why, but he picks it up.

"Hello?" he says.

"Merry Christmas, Jeff," says the voice on the other line.

"Ok. Same to you. Bye."

"Got a bit of a monster problem?"

"You might say that. But anyone with Tiktok can see that, right?"

"It's Ed. Ted and I are waiting for you in the parking lot of some place called 'Piggly Wiggly.' We have weapons and a couple others to help."

"Ed, why would I want to come with you? I saw what that thing is. No thanks. I trust y'all to take care of this one."

"No choice, I'm afraid."

The phone sounds like it's being run over by a truck made of fabric and then another voice comes across.

"Jeff," says the new voice. "Ted here. You and Gerald really should come along with us. We need two local, trustworthy yokels to back up that this was just a messed-up bird or something."

"Tedward, you fucker, it's already all over social media."

"That was a guy in a costume that decided to use an escaped bird from an exotic pet dealer as a way to kill people and start a new cryptid tale."

"You guys ever think that if your cover

stories were just a little better you may not have so many people who don't believe you?"

"Either way. Do it, or I guess we can make it so you two get arrested."

"Better than being dead."

"Jesus, you're really going to make me resort to the whole 'I'll kill everyone you love,' thing? Alright. We'll make sure your wife and grandkids are dead and the news says it was by your hands, THEN you'll go to prison."

"Yeah, yeah, see you in five."

Jeff hangs up the phone and shakes his head. Thanks to Bluetooth sending the call through the car stereo he knows Gerald heard.

"Tedward is a real prick, you know that?"

ELEVEN
Dig 'Em Up

There isn't an airport in Point Pleasant, WV. There never has been, and probably won't be. There are some flyovers from Columbus and Charleston. Across the bridge in Gallipolis there's a small runway.

But nothing you can use to fly in to for anything important.

There are nine people currently running as fast as they can across snow covered pavement who would probably disagree. Each swoop from above sounds like a low flying jet. Each one has a following of wind that hits as if it were a flying baseball team.

Jessica runs beside Lance as he carries Camry.

Chris is already in a giant concrete pipe waving at the others.

The five guys who got out of the truck are behind them.

The creature swoops down and shrieks at the group. It could drop all of its weight on one of them and make quick work of the poor sap. Truth be told, it's a little afraid. These five men got out of a vehicle that had one of those rods his father hurt him with. One of those rods that shoots pain and smoke.

He isn't looking to feel that pain again.

Damien Casey

The physical pain is one thing, but he feels the anguish of losing his father all over again when he sees the rod. One single tube made of metal with the worst of intentions can ruin a family and break a heart in two in his mind.

"Spuds!" yells one of the men. "Hurry the fuck up!"

"I'm tryin'!" Yells the man known as Spuds.

Jessica jumps down into the ditch and rolls into the pipe. She turns around fast and grabs Camry from Lance.

Lance jumps down and falls forward into the mud; his shoes acting like cinderblocks.

Another man's foot lands in the snow and mud beside his face splashing it all over him. The man screams and Lance watches his feet levitate. He stands up and stumbles into the pipe. He runs right into another large guy who grabs him to help him balance.

"Fuckin' spuds," says the voice Lance recognizes as Randall.

"Where'd Ethan go?" asks another voice.

"Ethan wear Nikes?" asks Lance.

"Yeah," says Randall. "Jaxon over there," Randall points to the other man, "told him it was a shit idea in case we had any running."

"Saw those Nikes levitating. Your guy was floating."

Camry is crying hard. Jessica holds her close and tries to comfort her. Chris is walking down the tunnel using the flashlight on his phone.

"Anyone got any signal?" Jaxon asks.

Red Ice

"Shit," says Randall, "not out here we ain't. Gotta get closer to town."

A body drops down onto the road ahead of them. It's Ethan. He's screaming and crying while grabbing his ankle. The bone is broken through the skin and grinding across the ground as he crawls closer to the pipe. He makes it to the ditch and Randall plans to step out and grab him.

The creature lands on Ethan's back and lifts him up into the air again. This time the flight is short, and Ethan comes falling back to Earth with a thud from around twenty feet above.

"Goddamn," says Randall. "Fuckin' thing is using him as bait. Why won't it come in here?"

"Hey!" A voice shouts from the other side of the road. "I got my walkie from work still! You forget yours too, Jax?"

"Spuds!" yells Jax out of the opening. "You shut the fuck up! I got Randall in here with me and he's bound be pissed!"

"Turn the thing on," says Randall. He snatches the walkie from Jaxon. "Spuds, you ol fuckin' potato. You got Liam there?"

"Yeah, he's here. He's crying and shit."

"Goddamn, Liam." Randall doesn't say this into the walkie. He just puts his head against it and sighs. "Guy with a name like that. No wonder."

"You still there?"

"Yeah."

"That thing came in after us. It opened its

wings, and something popped. It flew out real fast. I think it's too scared to come in now."

"Sounds about right."

"What about Aaron?"

Randall looks out at his friend on the road. He's just barely dragging his body along.

"I think he's being used as bait."

"Goddamn horror movie trope," says Lance.

Lance and Randall look out from the pipe. They turn their heads skyward and see the creature doing low circles. It's waiting for one of them to come out for their friend.

"You know," says Lance. "This gimmick has been done to death. But I'll be damned if it isn't scary as fuck to be a part of."

Aaron rolls over on the road and pulls a handgun from his jacket. He pops off one shot skyward before the bulk of the creature is on him. It lifts him five feet into the air and rips his flesh away in chunks. Claws and teeth work in unison like a hockey team to spread Aaron's blood all over the snow.

"Hey, Spuds," says Randall. "No fucking gunshots."

"Yeah," says Spuds. "No joke."

The creature tosses the remains of their friend into the air and leaps over to the ground above the other pipe. It starts digging at the ground like it can punch through the concrete and get the guys out.

"Fuckin' things trying to dig up a tater,"

Red Ice

Randall says while laughing.

"What do we do?" asks Jessica.

"There's just a bunch of dirt down there," says Chris. "It looks like they gave up building the thing."

"It was supposed to be a bridge," says Randall. "Pipe was gonna go under for wildlife."

"Oh," says Jessica. "That would have been nice." She rolls her head sarcastically. Maybe this is what they deserve as a species? She thinks of all the deer, raccoons, Opossum, dogs and cats. All of them turned to smears on the concrete because people have to get somewhere faster. Couldn't even be bothered to finish the thing that could slow the slaughter. *Maybe this thing is nature sorting us out?* She thinks. *Maybe it's just another one of our fuck ups.*

The creature gives up and flies across the road. It lands in front of the pipe opening so fast that Randall falls backward. It stands solid at the opening hissing and screaming. It behaves as though an invisible barrier is in front of it.

Randall stands up and brushes himself off. He flips the thing off and says, "I'm gonna kill you, you giant insect mother fucker."

The creature just continues to scream into the pipe.

"How long before it gets brave enough to come in here?" Lance asks as the thing launches back into flight.

"Probably too soon," says Chris.

Jessica holds Camry closer.

They can hear the sound of *Rudolph the Red Nosed Reindeer* playing from both cars in the road. Lance thinks his instinct to hop in one of those when the thing first swooped down may have been right. No sooner had they all touched flat ground from the wreckage had the thing started its attack. The first five missed, sending the thing flying into the open air. From then on it was like it knew they were on an open road, and it could take its time.

Now it flies overhead like a kid who played with food too long and missed a meal. It shrieks its frustration. Every now and again a piece of one of the cars will come flying at their pipe. If it isn't theirs, then Spuds is saying it's happening there.

The thing is throwing a temper tantrum.

"Who names their kid Spuds, anyway?" says Camry.

"It's his nickname," says Randall. "On account of he looks like a giant potato."

"You're not very nice. I don't like being stuck here with you."

"Yeah? Well, I don't like being in here with y'all either. Fuck you, little girl."

"Wow. You told a kid off. What an accomplishment."

Lance grins and nods. This is his daughter. He's never been prouder.

Red Ice

TWELVE
Don't Fear the Reaper

When Tyler signed up for the Marines, he didn't think he'd be in The Middle of Nowhere, West Virginia, population eighteen, riding in the back of a black van loaded up with every rapid-fire weapon the military could possibly place on a human. He wasn't going to complain though. He joined because he thought *Starship Troopers* was bad ass.

Now here he was, on a genuine mission. There's not really any conceivable way that they were going to actually fight aliens like those two guys said. They probably meant ILLEGAL aliens and fucking loser ass Eric misunderstood. He was for sure this was some Hopkinsville thing. Why else are they getting put on airplanes and flown into a winter covered Appalachian nowhere a week before Christmas?

Was it that soon?

Who knows?

Time is a flat circle and all that.

He got engaged before he left so that he knew Janet wasn't going to leave him.

Those are just words though, right?

They were for Tyler.

He slept with every piece of tail he could find over the past year. Stationed out of North

Red Ice

Carolina, home all the way out in Nevada. He didn't have to worry about anyone finding out. He wondered if that Cheryl chick from last night was blowing his phone up. Jokes on her, that number expires at the end of the month.

Thank God for prepaid.

"I haven't ever seen any snow," says Eric looking out a window.

The hills roll by and the other five men in the van seem nervous. Eric and Tyler are fine. They laughed the whole flight over about UFOs.

"You really think it's green aliens?" asks one marine Tyler never learned a name for.

"Yeah, man," says Eric. "They grey now though, you know?"

"Quite literally?"

"Oh yeah. Quite literally."

"You think they got alien tits?" Tyler asks.

No one answers because the sound of gunfire and screams gets louder. They all look at each other in anticipation.

A bullet flies through the front window. The driver falls forward onto the steering wheel sending the van careening into a ditch. Two of the six guys scream as the van rolls, the others clench their teeth and brace.

When the van stops moving, Tyler slides the side door open. It's positioned above them. A massive taloned hand reaches in and grabs the alien guy by his head. He flies out of the opening and up into the air somewhere around sixty feet before crashing back onto the van.

The top half of his body slides into the van as he gurgles blood from his mouth like foam.

The hand reaches in for another person that can be thrown like a wadded-up ball of foil. Gunfire hits its body, and it screams before launching into the air like a rocket.

Tyler kicks open the van's back doors. Eric rolls out in front of him.

Tyler looks back and sees a massive humanoid shape dive into the open door on top of the van. The last three men inside scream and shoot their guns.

The gunfire finally stops. Tyler and Eric stand back against back and look around. The only thing they see is chaos. At least five vans are spread out across the road. Body parts cover the asphalt.

Another van speeds along the road from the other direction and Tyler runs to it. He hears a voice screaming and looks to his left. Inside a concrete pipe a woman is yelling and pointing behind him.

He sees six Marines just like him get out of the van ahead of him and point guns in his direction. He dives to the ground and rolls so he can see behind him. He watches as Eric's body dances, the dance influenced by endless gunfire. His body is thrown at the van by the winged creature behind him. Eric's body hits one man full in his mass.

Tyler stands up and runs toward the van,

toward an escape route of any kind.

He hears *Rudolph the Red-Nosed Reindeer* begin to play loudly from the speakers of every vehicle on the road. Up ahead one of the other men is lifted into the air. His body slams against the ground beside Tyler. All of the air leaves the body at the same time as the blood and bones.

Another is lifted as the gunfire starts again. This man smashes to the ground in front of him. Tyler looks up and begins shooting into the snowfall. The creature screams out; it sounds like a car slamming on its brakes at a hundred miles per hour.

A bullet hits him in the shin. Bone and meat blow out the back of his calf. He falls down screaming in pain.

Up ahead, the last four Marines move forward in formation.

Bullets fly overhead as Tyler crawls along the asphalt. Gravel fills his wound with each inch he travels. Two of the men grab him under his arms and drag him backward.

One of the men shooting suddenly stops firing; seconds later his screaming gets closer and closer from above before he smashes against the ground

Rudolph plays on.

One of the men dragging Tyler is taken into the air. He doesn't release his grip and Tyler is stuck between the sky and the ground in a demented game of tug of war.

The sound of a bullet being fired almost deafens Tyler and he slams against the ground. He looks up and sees blood trickle from the hand of the man who was holding him.

Someone shot the man's hand to save Tyler's life.

A handgun is shoved in his hand.

"Shoot that thing if it gets low!" a man yells in his ear.

Tyler is dragged away again. This time by one man as the other fires away at the thing flying through the air. His head hits the concrete as he's dropped beside the sliding door of the van.

The man who was dragging him is now standing both without a head and a future. The man who was shooting is laying on the ground with the other's head smashed into his.

The creature lands on the ground beside Tyler. He pleads with it under his breath to leave him alone. It stretches out one talon and stabs it into his stomach.

The van door slides open, a man in a suit is pointing small torch at the creature. He pulls the trigger and flames shoot from the nozzle. Flaming gas falls down onto Tyler's face and chest. He feels his clothes catch fire and his whole world is pain and the smell of burning skin.

The creature flies away so fast that the talon pulls Tyler into the air for half a second. He crashes down to the ground and rolls into a small water filled ditch. He feels the mud and melted snow filling his wounds.

He claws his way up the side of the ditch. Every movement is pure agony. The creature has seemingly vanished.

When he peaks his head over the rim of the ditch, he's staring down the barrel of a handgun.

"I'm sorry this had to happen to you, soldier," says a voice behind the weapon. "Let me end your misery."

Tyler's brain doesn't even have the time to process a thought before a bullet passes through.

THIRTEEN
Escape Un-Plan

"Y'all see any of that, or just hear the fucking ruckus like us?" Spuds voice comes across the walkie.

"Just heard it," says Randall.

They did see a guy run by the tunnel getting chased by the creature as it did its best jet fighter impersonation while it was trying to catch its running victim, but not any of the gunfire that they heard.

A lot of screaming too.

Like, a LOT of screaming.

Camry has her ears covered by Jessica as Chris tries to pull up any Meghan Trainor song he can on his phone to calm the girl.

"Ok," says Lance. "I don't know what it is… but we have to do something."

"Thing isn't always going to be afraid of the tunnel," says Randall.

"It is now, so let's just wait it out," says Jax.

"Yeah?" asks Jessica. She's helping Camry to her feet, so both are standing up. "It sounded like the whole army just got demolished by weirdo bug man."

"Mothman," says Chris.

"I don't care if it's Jeff Goldblum dressed as Brundlefly. The thing is an absolute menace. I don't think we're getting by it with fists and

Red Ice

foul language."

"I'm not allowed to use foul language," says Camry. "I won't be able to help at all."

Randall shakes his head and punches the side of the concrete tunnel. He started this trip to torment Jessica a little for the scene at the bar, but his heart and mind can't take the danger the child is in. He thinks if he had wings, he'd fly up there and beat the shit out of this thing himself.

Lance feels the same rage. He feels like he's failed his daughter. First, he failed her when he couldn't keep the marriage together. Now he's failed her here and it may cost her life. He tries to shake these thoughts away. He knows they're about as real as he thought the weird bug man was three days ago.

Rudolph the Red-Nosed Reindeer plays from the walkie speaker. Lance and Randall step back instinctively.

It lands in front of the entrance again. Small high-pitched noises leave its throat as it runs its fingers along the concrete lip. Stretching one arm into the hole, it jerks it back quickly. It places one foot inside the tunnel, testing the water.

Lance sighs. His body language changes from "yeah, we have a chance," to "damn, we're dead," in two and a half seconds.

The thing ducks its head into the tunnel and screams before jumping back out. It slams its hands against the concrete and paces back and forth. Finally, it steps inside fully.

Randall can't figure out how much money he'd bet on it, but he was sure if someone asked him to bet on the facial expression the creature made, he'd win if he said a smile.

Camry starts crying as Lance steps in front of the group. She knows her dad isn't letting anything get to her unless it goes through him. But she can see that the thing he's trying to stop is twice his size and could probably rip right through him in five seconds.

Lance pulls his fist back, winding up all the strength he can. He punches the creature in the mouth. The impact sounds like a handgun going off and the thing leaps out of the tunnel.

Lance feels a sense of pride until he sees the two guys standing outside of the tunnel holding handguns.

"Shit," says Randall. "Spuds and fuckin' Liam to the rescue."

Before anyone can reply, Liam's head is separated from his body. Blood spews like a backed-up hose. Spuds looks to the sky and starts shooting.

"Yall gotta go!" Spuds yells. "That SUV is almost here."

Lance grabs Camry and runs to the entrance. Something in his gut tells him this was the right decision.

He climbs out of the ditch in time to see the back door of an SUV open.

Jeff is sitting there with his arms

outstretched.

Lance hands him Camry and turns around to help the others. Jessica and Chris crawl in, Lance follows and slams the door behind him.

From the other side of the SUV, Gerald jumps out and starts shooting at the thing above. He runs to the back and opens the trunk letting Randall and Jax in. He slams the hatch and gets back in.

"Come on, Spuds!" yells Randall from the back.

Spuds turns to run out of the ditch, but the previously removed head of his friend slams into the front of his nose, crushing it.

The SUV leaves black marks as it speeds away.

FOURTEEN
Mashed Taters

Imagine waking up making eye contact with one of your best friends. Now, imagine that friend's head isn't attached to their body. Then, imagine that you're lying down in the middle of an asphalt road while snow falls on you and him.

This is reality for a man named Spuds.

He rolls over and stands to his feet. He runs his hand across his shattered nose and wipes away the blood that has started to solidify there.

He looks up to the sky to see if that giant bug man is still flying around waiting to swoop down and take off his head as easy as a seagull fishing. He didn't even notice Liam's head was gone until he turned to see him falling over into the snow-covered hillside of that ditch.

Now what?

He sees the headlights of his would-be rescuers disappearing in the distance. He shoots them the bird with his left hand.

Y'all don't even get the good hand, y'all get the hand I wipe my ass with, he thinks.

Behind him, there's a thud. Melted snow splashes against his back.

"Fuckin' just my luck," Spuds says.

He thought they were all safe when that

Red Ice

weirdo's voice came across the walkie.

Some of them are; just not the guy who was supposed to be the hero.

Guy said to distract it long enough for them to get the SUV there.

The other group couldn't hear him; too far away.

He slowly turns around to face the creature. It stands at full height; its breathing seems labored. *Anyone would be after being shot about a million times*, Spuds thinks. He looks over the things body and notices there isn't a single bullet hole or scratch. Spuds shakes his head and tries to find the words to negotiate with an indestructible bug man.

"Hey," he says. "It doesn't have to be like this. It does not have to be like this."

The thing opens its wings and lets out a shriek while it steps forward. It towers at least three-foot above Spuds. Its breath coming down with the snow as a song about an outcast reindeer provides the soundtrack from the speakers of every crashed car.

"You know," Spuds starts. "People always forget about that one reindeer. What's his name? Goddamn it. This is from a movie. Hold on. Olive! They always forget about Olive. You know? Olive the other reindeer, used to laugh and call him names…"

The thing takes another few steps toward him as he backs up. It isn't in any hurry and could end this right here, but it wants to play games. It's tapped into some ancient code in its DNA. Something that was put there but never explored. The thrill of the hunt. The love of bloodshed. The hunger for fear and mutilation. Somewhere deep down inside, despite Arthur's best wishes, this thing was made to kill. It was made to be the world's deadliest soldier.

Spuds can see that in the red eyes that burrow under his skin. He can feel the thing processing how it wants to kill him. How long does it want to take? How much pain will it inflict?

He bends down and makes a snowball. He chucks it at the thing. It hits it in the face. The creature screams again not falling for the trap. Spuds was hoping if he pissed it off bad enough it may end this quickly but the pain shooting through his broken shin says otherwise.

It moved fast after it shrieked. Covered the distance in half a second. It struck its foot out hard and shattered all of the bones in Spud's shin sending him falling backward.

He pulled himself along with his hands. Pieces of wet gravel embedding themselves into his palms.

He gave up eventually and just lay there. He knows he isn't going to make it and this fucking thing is making a game out of his misery. *Fuck this*, he thinks, *at least it won't get whatever sick pleasure it's getting from this if I give up*.

His head lays flat against the asphalt. He

closes his eyes so he can't see whatever is coming. He feels a kick in his left slide and then air traveling below him. He slams down hard into a snow filled ditch. His arm bent back awkwardly as he flailed in the sky, snapping on impact.

Still, he fights through the pain and refuses to let the thing see he's terrified of death.

He doesn't know what comes after the pain, but he knows it has to be better than having a broken arm and leg lying face down in a pile of snow.

He feels a weight on the back of his head and closes his eyes. He feels the talons of the thing's foot scraping the side of his head. The pressure from above starts to increase. The last thing he hears or feels is a slight cracking in his skull.

FIFTEEN
Trapped by the Wards

"I can't believe we left Spuds like that," says Randall from the back.

"Your friend was dead," says Ted.

"Who the fuck are these guys anyway, Jeff? Gerald?"

"This is Edward," Jeff says nodding at the driver. "And this irritating sack of shit is Tedward."

"Tedward?" asks Lance.

Camry screams out from the backseat. All eyes are directed to the front window just in time to see two red dots fly over the car.

"Son of a bitch bastard won't let us go," says Ed. He pushes the gas pedal down. The sound of *Rudolph the Red-Nosed Reindeer* fills the SUV. Ted reaches over to turn it down and the volume doesn't work. He punches the radio trying to get it to stop; instead, it switches over to *Frosty the Snowman.*

"It's too loud and crowded in here!" yells Chris.

Gerald rolls down his window, he points his sidearm out and fires six quick shots into the sky.

"I think I hit it," Gerald says.

The sound of a body landing atop the moving vehicle is too similar to the sound of something tragic about to happen for Jeff.

"Turn left!" Jeff yells.

The SUV whips around a corner at top speed. For half a second it tips on two wheels, the impact of the vehicle coming back shakes the thing on the roof off a little.

Camry looks at the roof; her eyes following the sound of claw digging into metal.

Jessica grabs her and pulls her closer.

The creature's face fills the front windshield. Ed slams on the brakes and sends it sailing forward. It skids across the blacktop.

Jessica cracks a smile watching it. She thinks back to every cartoon that shows someone sliding face first on the ground. The creature's legs looked the same. They angled back, making its body resemble a scorpion. She even hears the car brake sound from Loony Tunes.

The thing plants its hands on the concrete and pushes itself up into a squat. It turns and faces the car; its body looks unaffected from its surprise sledding trip.

It spreads its wings and lets out a shriek. Its form radiates beams like a sun made of pissed off and violence. Its wings seem to glow.

Everyone in the car screams out. Fear fills the vehicle like water in a bathtub.

"Bright the fucking thing!" yells Randall.

Ed flips the switch lighting it up in more wattage than every Christmas tree in the county.

It leaps into the air.

The sound of *Frosty the Snowman* on the radio slowly fades away. The brights seemingly scared it off long enough to make an escape.

"Ok," says Gerald. "Now what?"

"Arthur had a tranquilizer gun with some poison darts. That's what we were looking for that day. Firepower used to work, but that's things gotten stronger. I think we all knew that would happen as it aged. Darts will stop it."

"What about us?" asks Jessica.

"Well," says Ed. "Sorry to say it but you're all coming along until we can neutralize the situation and debrief you about what to say."

"I'll tell you what I'm going to say," Chris says. "I'm going to say I saw the Mothman."

Ted pulls a gun from his jacket and points it back at Chris' face.

"No," Ted says, "I don't think you will."

"No," says Chris, "I don't think I will. Probably a gas leak or something is what happened."

SIXTEEN
It's not a Costume It's a Way of Life

The steps outside of Arthur's house have been untouched since the police left. There's a layer of snow and ice coating the wooden porch. One of the idiots on scene didn't shut the front door all the way so the wind blew it open. The living room is half covered in snow; all of the furniture has a thin layer of frost coating it like a glazed donut.

The stairs crack as the weight of a man and a woman walk up them. The porch sounds like a pile of breaking glass as the ice shatters and the wood groans.

Laurel Addy didn't have any kids. A fact that makes it kind of odd that she's referred to as a MILF by her boyfriend, Tony. He says, "it's because she has that look, you know?" Then he will go on to explain that not all "MILF" pornstars even have kids. They just have a look. Instead of the girl next door look, it's like your friend's hot mom. The mom who cooks French toast AND waffles when you stay over because she isn't sure which one you like better. The mom who sort of forgets how her thick thighs and DD cup bra size makes her son almost get into fights daily because one of his friends inevitably creates some gross ass

Damien Casey

fantasy about French toast and sex.

Laurel loves it. She loves it so much she plays it up on her YouTube channel, "MILF Ghost Hunters," where she introduces herself as, "the MILF without kids."

Tony said that may be a little weird to do, but the viewers didn't care. They keep tuning in because every time they see a "ghost" the camera is pointing at Laurel's frontside when she jumps.

YouTube is easy.
Men are easy.

Make your boobs bounce just a little, and BLAMMO! you've gotten one of those golden YouTube plaques.

Ghosts and tits.
Specters and breasts.
Boo-bies.

All of these names are ones that haunt her at night because she knows they would have been better titles for the show. Boo-bies especially would have played into her character more than the title she uses now that sounds slightly like a PornHub parody of a ghost hunting show.

She's not here to fuck ghosts.

She's here to pretend to see something, jump a little, get some good backside footage, and watch the money come rolling in faster than middle aged dads showing up for a half off New Balance shoe sale.

Instead, she settled for calling her fan base

Red Ice

The Boo-bies. Works out nice when slapped on a tank top that other "MILFs" are buying.

Like the woman in Friday the 13th part 5 who has one line, gets naked, then dies... Laurel has made a living and a cult following because of two pieces of anatomy she didn't even have to work for.

The internet rules.

"Hey, Boo-bies!" She exclaims into the camera as she enters the front door. "It's me, Laurel... and as you can see, I'm sort of a MothMilf tonight! We're here at a house in Point Pleasant, West Virginia where one of my viewers claims to have seen the world famous Mothman more than once. Shout out to LettuceLover69 for the info!"

"What does that even mean?" asks Tony.

"Huh? What does what mean?"

"Lettuce lover 69?"

"What do YOU think it means, Tony?"

"I don't know if you should be saying that name on the show."

"Why, exactly, is that?"

"I don't know. Could mean anything."

"Tony, shut up and film."

She does a spin for the camera showing her full outfit. She's wearing all black spandex, antennas on her head, and red goggles.

"What exactly is a MothMilf?" She asks the camera. "Well, Laurel the MothMilf was created in a lab. Created to be the perfect host for the most perfect ghost hunting show. She was made to be the picture perfect MILF so that all of you Boo-bies out there can picture what it would be like to have a night with me and some ghosts, but then getting to wake up to a breakfast of bacon and sausage links because I wasn't sure which you liked better and I'm just trying to be a good mommy."

"Ok," says Tony. "The mommy thing was a bit odd…"

"People like it! You know this! You interrupted me before I could even make the innuendo about sausage links! Jesus, Tony!"

"Ok, well, sorry I don't like my girlfriend being sexualized like this."

"You're literally filming the show. You've filmed the show the whole time it's been a thing. You never care about any of that when I'm buying dinner."

"Yeah, but since you started that OnlyFans…"

"Where I'm never nude, by the way."

"Yeah… well… some of the boys at work bought it. They're a little pissed you AREN'T naked. They're always picking on me and trying to force me to show them pictures of you because they paid for it with their monthly fee."

"Excuse me?"

"Yeah… they say at six bucks a month they should at least see a nipple. I don't even know that they care about both nipples. Just one."

"Tony… if you don't shut the fuck up right

Red Ice

now before you tell me you showed them pictures… I'm going to make sure that anyone who ever looks at you naked from here on out never sees a nipple again. That's right, because they will be left here after I rip them off with my bare hands."

"So…"

"Tony. I'm begging you to not say what you're about to say."

"I did show them…"

"Don't fucking say it, Tony."

"Well… they kinda had a point…"

"Don't you dare."

"If I paid for someone's spicy site and I don't get to see… you know…"

"Jesus Christ, what did you show them?"

"Just a couple pictures… the ones you sent in the Olaf onesie…"

"Ugh…"

"Ok… and maybe a few videos… they promised they'd delete them after they watched 'em though…"

"Delete them… did you fucking send them to their phones?"

"How else would they have it for… well… that's kinda awkward to talk about…"

Laurel takes three steps toward him. Her eyes radiate nothing but hatred, violence, and gonna kill a mother fucker. She stops before she reaches him and says, "there is someone in the doorway…"

Tony turns slowly and faces the figure.

Damien Casey

Whoever it is has to duck to come into the darkened house. The figure moves quick and quietly. Neither of them see where it goes but hear things falling off shelves.

The TV comes on and starts playing static with *Rudolph the Red-Nosed Reindeer* coming through faintly. A radio comes on and plays *Frosty the Snowman*. The music, mixed with the static of the TV create a modern technology-based Christmas hell in reality.

The glow of the TV shows the faint outline of the person standing beside it. The figure stands taller than any person Laurel has ever met. Its arms are thin and wiry, covered in grey skin. Its hands are massive, ending in clawed talons.

"What the fuck is that?" Asks Tony.

"Probably some other fucker that heard you were giving away pictures," Laurel says as she backs toward a doorway.

"Well, what do you want?" Tony takes a few steps forward. He reaches the thing and shoves it. Laurel shakes her head in fear; of course, Tony thinks it's a person he can fight.

He punches the thing in the face. When it doesn't react, he says, "you know what? I don't think I want to fight you anymore."

The music triples in volume, the lights in the house get so bright it's hard to see. The thing lets out a shriek and spreads its wings.

Laurel runs.

She can hear Tony's screams as she opens a

Red Ice

doorway to a set of stairs. She can hear liquid splattering against the floor above her as she makes her way through a darkened basement. The ground is dirt covered and cold. She turns on the flashlight on her phone and jumps in fear. Before her is a giant piglike face, it's pink with massive tusks. Its skin is covered in scars, warts, and random teeth poking through at spots teeth don't belong.

She falls on her ass and shines the light up at her new attacker. It's a mounted head. Some hunter's bad taxidermy job on a boar or something.

She shines the light along the wall and sees framed pictures of two girls with the strange creature. There's a picture of them with a creature that appears to be the Mothman. The label reads, "the girls and Lemmy."

She looks around more and sees the same pig creature covered in blood. It's in a room surrounded by the ripped apart bodies of soldiers. The two girls stand hand in hand; their eyes are completely black, their skin pure white. They faintly resemble something human, but also don't look anything like human beings.

She reaches over and touches the pig head, its plastic, a replica.

She looks around below it and finds another picture attached to a newspaper article titled, "Mysterious Photo Catches Strange Children with a Bizarre Pet." This one is grainy and looks like one of those pictures people say is proof of Bigfoot. It shows the outline of the two girls walking through a forest with the pink thing between them. Written below the picture, covering some of the article, "I hope the three of them are ok. I hope they also found better names than the ones I made up for them. They deserved to have names."

A loud crash and shriek from above causes her to lose her phone. The thing must not have noticed she slipped away.

She follows the light and finds it pointing to another picture. This one of a small green creature with massive teeth and ears. It's being pulled through a swirling hole in a white wall. Below it, someone has written, "travelers from another dimension?" Another picture shows a man and a giant ape like creature surrounded by what can only be described as frog people. She flips the picture over, the writing on the back reads, "captured at site CCHDF. Apparently, we're not the only dimension who have found this world…"

She drops the picture when the basement door flies open. She throws her phone away hoping to hide. She finds a cabinet and hides behind it. The legs of the creature are illuminated as it steps over her phone. Rudolph begins playing from the small speaker. She frantically searches for anything to defend herself with. She opens a cabinet door; light pours from inside. The whole basement looks like it's covered in lights, the one single cabinet

Red Ice

lighting everything up better than the sun.

The creature jumps back against the wall. Steam pours from its skin like it's being burnt. It leaps up the stairs and away from the light.

Laurel searches inside and finds a thing that looks like a shotgun but has a light at the end. She points it at the wall and pulls the trigger. Light shoots from the barrel like a flashlight being turned off and on, the spot on the wall steams like it's been burnt.

She sets the weapon aside and looks at the other item inside; a rifle and about six darts.

She runs her hand along the weapon but is distracted by shrieking from upstairs. A light passes through the stairwell that looks like the headlights of a car passing by. She can hear voices outside yelling at each other.

She grabs the light rifle and heads to the staircase. Laurel the MothMilf refuses to let anyone else die on her watch.

SEVENTEEN
Field Trip

Camry shivers when the cold air hits her. The weird guy named Tedward wouldn't let her and Jessica stay behind. He said something about them taking the car and leaving. Like she would do that to her dad. Besides, she never got her driver's license.

They walk up the stairs slowly and into the front door.

"Alright," says Edward. "You guys can wait here. Jeff, Gerald, let's go. Ted, you stay here."

"We're going too," says Randall showing his gun. Jaxon follows suit.

She's never been around this many guns in one room. She counts six. Her dad always said they should keep at least one gun in a safe in case they needed protection, but even that was a risk he wasn't comfortable with.

If it's in the safe, what can it do? She thinks. *Can it open the lock and walk around?*

"AHHHHHH! That fuckin' burns!" Yells Randall.

"Shit," says a woman's voice Camry doesn't recognize. "I thought you were that thing comin' back. Really hates this flashlight gun."

Without a voice to warn of it, or a sign, gunshots go off inside the house. It sounds like all six guns let loose upon the world to paint on

Red Ice

a canvas called who's to blame for gun violence in America with a shade of paint called NRA Red. Camry buries her face into Lance and Jessica as they squeeze her closer between them. Chris lays down on the ground and covers his ears. Ted leaves them like that and pulls his own gun to join the party.

***

Randall shakes his head, as quick as the thing appeared, it vanished. The bullets did absolutely nothing to it.

"Y'all," says Laurel. "Hey. Hi. How are you? It does NOT like this light gun thing. Lemme shoot it when it comes back."

"I'll take that," says Ed reaching for the gun.

Laurel slaps his hand away and then on the comeback motion slaps him across the face. Ed points his pistol in her face, she flips him the bird.

She pushes the gun away and says, "jokes on you, I'm the only one who can use it. Go ahead and kill me, Mr. Suit and Tie Man."

"I like you, Ms…"

"Addy. I don't much like you. Stop fucking around acting like because I'm the sexiest MothMilf you've ever gazed upon, that I can't shoot a gun."

"I was wonderin' why you were here," says Gerald.

"Had to rescue your sorry ass… and film a

new YouTube special. Sorry I'm pissy, I'm a little keyed up on account of Tony getting his ass killed."

"Oh my god," says Jaxon. "I'm so sorry."

"Eh, I'll be sad after I stop being pissed and feeling like I'm in a fever dream. Gerald, you look nice."

"Thanks."

Both of them blush a little at the compliments.

"Well holy fucking pumpkin spiced lattes in July," says Randall. "Let's stop standing around and talking so that we can find this dart gun and you two can go on a fucking date or something. Jesus H!"

"Oh! That's down here!"

They all make their way into the basement following Laurel's lead. Every flashlight on every cell phone lights the place up.

Jaxon screams as his light shines on the face of the boar.

They all shake their head in secondhand embarrassment.

Laurel opens the cabinet.

The light from inside illuminates the whole room.

"How did you find this?" asks Ed. "We searched down here."

"Apparently not good enough," says Jeff.

Ted steps forward and closes the cabinet. He hands Ed his gun and picks the wooden box up.

Red Ice

Jaxon leads the way up the stairs.

He freezes at the top like someone pushed the pause button on his life. His hands drop to his sides and start twitching. He turns to face the group but instead falls down the stairs.

They all watch in horror as he stops.

Where his face used to be are just giant claw marks.

They turn to look at the top of the stairs, the doorway is blacked out.

"Shit," says Ed before shooting at the thing with both pistols.

Ted sets down the cabinet and frantically opens it up.

Laurel points the light gun through the bodies in front of her and pulls the trigger. The things' foot lights up and starts to sizzle. It screams and runs away.

"Let's fucking move!" says Ed.

The stairs explode in front of them before they make it to the front door. They all fall back into the basement. The thing floats above the group with its wings spread wide. It looks like the angel of death and insects.

"There's a back door," says Randall as he turns to run.

They all follow along and head out of the back entrance.

Lance stops and points his gun at the thing. He fires a few shots to distract it hoping to buy some time.

Ted is the last one to come. He stops in

place and gets pulled backward. The cabinet flies from his hands and bursts on the concrete. His voice can be heard screaming all through the house.

Lance acts quick and grabs the gun and darts that flew out of it. He runs out of the door behind the rest of the group.

"Fuckin' thing got Tedward!" He yells as he catches up.

Ed stops running and turns back toward the basement.

"It's no use, Ed," says Jeff. "The only thing that hurts it is Laurel's gun."

"And I ain't giving it to you to go on a suicide mission over someone named Tedward," Laurel says.

Ed bows his head, says a few words none of them understand, and follows the group. They run around the front of the house yelling for the rest of the group.

***

When all the noise happened, Jessica shoved Camry into a toy box. Inside were plush reindeer and snowmen. It was honestly pretty comfortable. After all the screaming from the basement stopped, she heard people yelling for them to get to the car. She hears Jessica and Chris scream out. Rudolph begins to play loudly.

She thinks the car must be here, so she

stands up and opens the lid.

Jessica is lying on the floor trying to get back to her feet. The monster has Chris pinned against a wall with its arm pulled back, preparing for the killing blow.

Camry stands up and starts screaming and throwing toys at the thing. It drops Chris, spreads its wings, shrieks, and flies at her.

She feels herself being lifted off the ground and carried through the air. She sees her dad way down below on the ground screaming for help.

***

Jessica gets her feet under her and stumbles outside. Lance is on his knees crying while the rest of the group try to get him to the car. Chris runs out behind her and heads straight for the SUV.

Jessica stoops down beside Lance and wraps her arms around him.

"It didn't kill her," she says. "That means it must be messing with us, or it has some weird code of ethics against killing kids. Mothy Meyers or something."

Lance looks at her with tears streaming down his face and cracks a smile, albeit a small one.

"Let's go get her back," Jessica says. "Then we can kill that thing for fucking with us and go see all the Christmas lights like you

promised me."
    He nods and stands up.
    Together they load into the car.

EIGHTEEN
First Class

The town passes below.

Camry cries, the creature whimpers.

She thinks it sounds like the whines of her dog when he's been bad. Lil' Biscuit always whines like that when he pees or poops on the floor. He's trying to get you to feel bad for being upset with him.

But this thing has done worse than leaving a little turd on her mom's white carpet; this thing has made people not alive anymore.

She can't think of it as killing someone, that all seems too dark for her mind to comprehend right now.

It's all she can do to not cry and beg the thing to set her down. They're up as high as airplanes it feels like. She knows that isn't true, because she has to lift her feet away from trees here and there. But she feels like she's tied to the bottom of an airplane.

She starts humming Rudolph because she's nervous. The thing stops making those sounds and begins to lower their flight. Together they fly over passing cars that honk their horns as if they could do anything about what's happening.

She sees camera flashes go off all over.

She doesn't bother asking for help, she

knows no one can do anything right now.

They fly between buildings and through the downtown area before going back up high again.

She can see the lights over at Krodel Park up this high. She wonders if the thing is looking at the light display that was made in its image sitting beside the pond.

She starts humming louder.

She wants to be closer to the ground.

Their flight starts again, only this time they touch down on the first bridge out of town.

Traffic swerves, some slam on their brakes.

The sun is starting to rise, so these people must be on their way to jobs they hate to buy presents for the ones they love.

"Hey!" Yells the voice of a stranger. "What's all of this about? I'm already running late."

"Excuse me, sir," says Camry. "I would get back in your car. Please don't make him mad."

"Is this your dad? Some asshole in a suit?"

"No, sir. This is the Mothman."

"You've got to be shitting me. Move it asshole!"

He gets back in his car and slowly drives forward honking his horn. When the car is in reaching distance, the winged creature grabs the front and slings it into the air. The car splashes down into the river.

That was all it took. Every car on the bridge is either switching to reverse or trying to do a

Red Ice

U-turn.

    Camry sits down and leans her back against the concrete barricade. She hopes her dad knows where to look.

NINETEEN
Memories of Tomorrow

"I got all the roads closed," says Jeff. "I got the bridges cleared of people, told the other officers there was a crazy guy in a used costume from the Richard Gere movie holding a little girl hostage, AND I told them not to engage because the man wants to talk to the mother... Which is you, Jessica."

"Good work," says Ed. "Looks like small town police can still handle things when the need arises."

Jeff doesn't respond. He looks at Lance and rolls his eyes.

They're speeding down snow covered roads, going at least eighty. The tires start to lose traction, Ed mumbles "mother fucker," then the car straightens up like it's afraid of insults.

When they get to the bridge, Jeff flashes his badge and they're allowed to pass through. They have to stop about a quarter of the way up due to most of the drivers seeing a car get flung into the river one handed and saying, "nope," before running away.

Lance is the first out of the car.

The abandoned cars are playing some weird mashup of Frosty and Rudolph.

"Camry!" He yells over and over as he runs

Red Ice

up to the clearing. The creature is sitting on the concrete barricade staring out over the river. Camry is standing beside it leaning over and watching ice flow along the river.

Camry and the creature both turn to look at the source of the yelling. One smiles, the other hisses and flings saliva in every direction.

Laurel aims the light rifle toward the thing and Lance pushes the barrel down.

He makes eye contact with her and tries to telepathically tell her he wants to try this peacefully while his daughter is being held captive.

"Hey, Lemmy," says Ed. He walks cautiously toward the thing with his palms open. "Why don't you let the little girl go, then we can take you someplace else. Someplace you're familiar with. How does that sound?"

It hisses and takes two steps toward Ed. Ed takes the dart gun from Randall and points it at the thing. "Now come the fuck on," he says. "You're going with me whether you want to or not. You know this, I know this, Christ, even Gerald knows it."

Gerald shrugs and makes eye contact with the creature as if to say, "what're you gonna do, you know?"

It hisses again and steps forward.

Chris and Jessica take a few steps back away from the madness before Jessica remembers it's Camry out there. This isn't just Ed's mess now. This thing ruined her Hallmark Christmas movie moment and she's pissed.

"Chris," she says. "I'm about sick of Edward over here ruining our vacation."

"Me too," says Chris. "The very second I laid eyes on him I knew he was worse than whatever The Mothman was turning out to be."

Before they can move, Randall jumps toward Ed. He was clearly thinking the same thing, only his attempt fails. Ed throws him to the ground, shoots him in the arm with one of the darts and kicks him in the head.

Randall stands up and stumbles around like a drunk. He swings his fists at empty air. He takes the light rifle from Laurel and points it at Ed.

"I've had about enough of your shit, Edward," he says while stumbling.

"Keep pointing that thing at me," says Ed. "The poison in that dart could put the megalodon to sleep; you'll probably die."

No sooner than Ed says it, Randall stumbles forward. He shoots the light rifle. The beam hits Ed on the right shoulder setting his black jacket on fire.

Ed takes off the jacket and launches it at Randall.

It wraps around Randall's face. He begins screaming and trying to get the flaming piece of clothing away from him, but his body is moving sluggishly. He stumbles toward Camry, and everyone holds their breath expecting

Red Ice

disaster.

A hand grabs Randall by his leg and throws him into the sky. His body hits one of the beams on the bridge and splits in two before splashing down into the Ohio River.

Ed looks at the wound on his chest and groans. He looks at the spot where the light rifle landed. He can shoot this thing in the head and be done with it.

The gun is gone.

Chris stands beside him with the barrel aimed right at his temple.

Ed moves quicker than any human being should be able to and steals the rifle from Chris' hand. He shoots it point blank at Chris face, but only singes his ear thanks to Jessica tackling him from behind.

He kicks Jessica hard in the face and rolls to his side. He points the gun at the rest of the group before realizing his awareness has put him in a bad spot.

A shadow falls over him and he looks into the eyes of the beast he has been sent here to bring back alive. He disregards those orders and points the rifle right at its face.

The mouth opens, and a weight slaps him in the side sending him skidding across the concrete.

The thing launches into flight, Ed shoots the rifle at it in the sky. The beams miss each time.

To Lance this looks like someone trying to

play *House of the Dead* at the arcade and failing miserably. He takes his chance and runs to Camry.

The Mothman swoops down and knocks Jeff into Gerald. Their heads and chests collide leaving both dazed and out of breath.

The thing swoops back up into the air and then lands on Ed's chest with both feet. The sound is like a car being dropped into a pool of Jello and bones.

Ed screams out and drops the gun, he tries to reach for it as it slides all the way down the wet incline of the bridge.

Laurel chases after it like one of those people chasing a wheel of cheese down a hill.

He feels the back of his skull bouncing on the concrete like it's being dribbled by Shaquille O'Neal in his prime. His vision fades as he begins to hear cracking.

Lance feels his leg go out from under him. He falls to the ground hard and sees that one of Ed's arms was the projectile that took him out. The Mothman stands over him. They're eye to eye as it bends down. He can smell its breath; he can feel the heat radiating from the gaping maw.

The lights on the bridge glow brighter and brighter until they burst, the stereos playing Rudolph and Frosty crackle and sizzle as they break apart.

Lance is lifted into the air and thrown hard against the barricade separating him from the river. He can't move his left arm and he's positive he heard something shatter in his chest.

The Mothman picks up Camry and moves to the barricade as if to take flight again.

Jessica has managed to pick up the dart gun, she fires two shots that land in the thing's back. It stumbles around and holds Camry over its head like it just scored the game winning touchdown and wants to celebrate by spiking the ball.

"You know Dasher and Dancer and Prancer and Vixen," sings Camry.

"Comet and Cupid and Donner and Blitzen." She's crying between every line, sniffling between every word.

The poison is sinking into The Mothman's blood stream. He starts to stumble around while lowering Camry.

"But do you," she sings and sniffles. "Recaaaallllllll."

She feels her feet touch the ground.

Inside Lemmy's head, because he's closer to Lemmy than a monster currently thanks to the poison taking the edge off his hurt rage, is a small boy singing the same song. He sees two parents looking at their children; one biological and one adopted. He sees the smiles of pride in those faces. He feels the love in the hug the boy gives him when he opens a box to find a plush Frosty inside. He feels the love he had for the boy when he found a stuffed Rudolph in his box.

"The most wonderful," again Camry sniffles. "Reindeer of alllllll."

She wipes a tear from Lemmy's face.

He roars out and shoves her away before leaping away.

Everyone watches as The Mothman soars over the barricade and out of site. They hear the splash as his massive body hits the water below.

Lance and Jessica hold Camry while Chris and Gerald go to see where the thing has gone.

Laurel walks up carrying the light rifle, she sees the danger is over. "Gerald," she says. "Please come hold me. I'm sorry about whatever happened in the past."

Gerald smiles and holds her as they both sit down on the concrete.

"Well," says Chris, "guess it's just us then, huh?" He says as he leans into Jeff. Jeff laughs and shrugs him off as the road is filled with red and blue lights.

TWENTY
A Year Later on the Hallmark Channel

The best Christmas lights are the ones that are synced to music. They're the only thing on Earth that can make any kind of music feel festive.

Seasons in the Abyss by Slayer? Festive.
Hit 'Em Up by Tupac? Festive.
No by The Subhumans? FESTIVE.

Just turn on those lights and let the holiday cheer shine through.

Camry finally figured out how to hook her Bluetooth to the giant musical display in the Gallipolis Park. She tuned it in and pushed play on her new favorite band, The Linda Lindas. Meghan Trainor was last year, this year it's punk or nothing.

She was hoping her dad and Jessica got her tickets to see them with Hot Water Music next year for her Christmas present. Actually, she knew they did. Not only was her uncle Chris good at hacking into light displays, but he knew all of Jessica's passwords. Plus, it was hard to deny when Camry noticed everyone saying they had to take the same day off in March... the same day that lined up with the show in Cincinnati...

"Wow," says Lance watching the lights.

"Great job. Try Gorgoroth next."

Jessica elbows him on the shoulder. She's about worn out of him constantly picking on her about her black metal phase. Forget to throw out one single Mayhem shirt and all of a sudden, your boyfriend thinks you're an asshole.

Camry just nods and laughs. She doesn't get why the joke is funny, but she likes to pretend. She switches the song Meghan Trainor's *White Christmas* and walks away with Chris. Some M-Train is still needed here and there.

"Hey, Jessica," says Lance. "You ever notice something we have in common with those Hallmark movies?"

"Oh!" says Jessica. "Is it because we killed The Mothman and participated in a massive government coverup? You're a single dad with a daughter who takes life too seriously. I'm a single young woman who thinks Christmas is magical and wants to spend all of her time in this small town at Christmas. Are you about to finish the story and ask me to marry you?"

Lance sighs and goes down on one knee.

"Lance," Jessica says making him stand up. "I'll say yes if you stand up and stop looking like an asshole."

Epilogue
A Year Before Proposal on the Banks of the Ohio River

"Seeing anything?" A man's voice speaks in the darkness.

"Not a goddamned thing," says a different voice.

"Tracking shows it's right around here."

"Was tracking right with that other one?"

"That giant sheep asshole? Hell, no it wasn't."

"Then why do you- FUCK!"

The sound of two darts firing from a rifle leads the events. A massive grey being with wings and red eyes stumbles along on the mud before falling down face first.

"Hey," says a voice. "We got 'im. What do you want us to do?"

A walkie goes off in the darkness.

The voice on the other end is calculated, deadly.

"Take it back. Put it with the other ones. We'll round all of these things up if it's the last thing I do."

Damien Casey

THANKEE

Breanna Spencer for not putting up any Santa junk.

Mercedes Mone/Varnado for being my hero.

I genuinely try to thank people and show my appreciation for them daily.

If I love you and appreciate you, you know I do.

Please, save me from forgetting your name and write it below.

Thank you,

_____

Also, dear reader, you mean the entire world to me.

You've chosen my weird Xmas book over so many other books to read for however long it took to read it.

For that, I am forever grateful and hope I didn't waste your time.

As with the others, please write your name below.

_____

K THX

About Damien Casey

Damien Casey really likes Christmas.
He doesn't like Santa.
Like, not at all.
It's honestly a phobia.
Kind of like his other phobia.
The one where he's afraid Earth's gravity will reverse.
Then we all fall upwards toward the sky.
So, in summary...
Santa=BAD
Falling toward the sky=BAD

ALSO BY DAMIEN CASEY

Coffin Dodger

When your favorite actors aren't acting, they're dealing with ghost-snakes, giant crocodiles, spiders with human faces, and cults kidnapping them. One of these cults kidnaps a group of actors from a cult classic horror series. This cult forces the group to play a game where they have to face their biggest fears in order to gain eternal life. They don't even want eternal life. It's all pretty inconvenient.

28 Days Sassier
It's a post-apocalyptic Bigfoot book.

Damien Casey

Heartburn

Ten blind dates in ten days...
How bad could it be?
Unfortunately, Dana Ripley is about to go on
the bad date carousel.
Heartburn, a romantic comedy for the dating
app age.

Red Ice

PUP

Jen Maroni lives in a small Ohio town with a
bit of a werewolf problem.
That doesn't even cover her new demon BFF
and Satan cooking omletes.